A Tiger for Breakfast

Narinder Dhami
Illustrated by Chris Corr

A & C Black • London

White Wolves series consultant: Sue Ellis,
Centre for Literacy in Primary Education

This book can be used in the White Wolves Guided Reading
programme by readers who need a lot of support in Year 2

The rights of Narinder Dhami and Chris Corr to be identified
as the author and illustrator of this work has been asserted by them
in accordance with the Copyrights, Designs and Patents Act 1988.

ISBN 978-1-4081-2653-0

A CIP catalogue for this book is available from the British Library.

This book is produced using paper that is made from wood
grown in managed, sustainable forests. It is natural, renewable
and recyclable. The logging and manufacturing processes conform
to the environmental regulations of the country of origin.

Printed and bound in China by C&C Offset Printing Co.

Chapter One

It was a hot, dusty day in India. The sun shone down on the flat green fields and the sky was blue.

Ram the farmer was digging his field.

Suddenly, a tiger jumped out of the trees. "My name is Bali," it said. "And I'm very, *very* hungry. So now I'm going to eat you!"

"Please don't do that!" cried Ram.
"My wife has a pretty white cow at home.
It will taste much better than me."

"Then bring me that cow," growled Bali. "And if you don't, I'll eat you, your wife and all your children!"

Chapter Two

Ram ran home as fast as he could.

His wife Reeta was in the yard. She was milking the pretty white cow.

Ram told Reeta what had happened.

Reeta was very angry.

"You want me to give my pretty white
cow to that greedy tiger?" she said. "Never!"

"But if I don't, Bali will eat you and me and all our children!" said Ram.

"We'll see about that!" said Reeta.
She told Ram to go and get their
horse.

But when he returned, Reeta had gone.

Chapter Three

Instead, there was a man in the yard.
Ram looked puzzled.

"Don't worry, Ram. It's only me!"
laughed Reeta. "I'm wearing your turban
and your clothes."

"Why are you doing that?" asked Ram.

"You'll see!" Reeta replied.

She got on the horse and rode out
to the field.

Ram and the pretty white cow came with them.

"I hope I find a tiger today," Reeta said loudly. "I haven't eaten a tiger for days. And I do love a tiger for breakfast!"

Chapter Four

When Bali heard the farmer's wife,
he was very frightened. He ran off into
the forest to hide.

There, he bumped into a tiger called Tikkoo.

"Hey," Tikkoo growled. "Look where you're going!"

"Run!" Bali shouted. "That man in the field eats tigers for breakfast!"

21

Tikkoo peeped through the trees.
He saw Reeta sitting on her horse.

"You fool," Tikkoo laughed. "That is the farmer's wife dressed like a man. Now, let's go and eat *them* for breakfast!"

23

"How do I know you are telling the truth?" Bali asked. "What if you run off and leave me?"

"We'll tie our tails together," said
Tikkoo. "Then I can't go anywhere
without you."

So that's what the tigers did.

Chapter Five

Ram and Reeta were laughing about how they'd tricked Bali.

Suddenly, they saw *two* tigers run out of the trees.

"That's Tikkoo, the biggest tiger in the land!" said Ram. He was very frightened.

"Hello, Tikkoo, my friend," called Reeta. "I see you've brought Bali for my breakfast. He's a nice fat tiger, and I'm *so* hungry. You can have my pretty white cow in return!"

Bali looked at Tikkoo. "You tricked me," he growled.

"No, I didn't," said Tikkoo. "She's lying!"

But Bali wouldn't listen. He ran off
into the forest, pulling Tikkoo with him.

Reeta and Ram laughed. Then they went home with their pretty white cow.